Amazing!

by

Hilary McKay

Illustrated by Mike Phillips

You do not need to read this page –
just get on with the book!

First published in 2008 in Great Britain by
Barrington Stoke Ltd
18 Walker Street, Edinburgh, EH3 7LP

www.barringtonstoke.co.uk

Reprinted 2008

ISBN: 978-1-84299-530-3

Printed in Great Britain by Bell & Bain Ltd

AUTHOR ID

Name: Hilary McKay

Likes: Millions of things! Books, cats, honey, letters from readers (hint, hint), real music, apples, swimming in cold water, chocolate coated ginger biscuits, trees.

Dislikes: Putting things away, litter, loud TV, hot rooms, being told what to think.

3 words that best describe me:
Untidy, happy, hopeful!

A secret that not many people know:
I am, and always have been, a VERY slow reader!

ILLUSTRATOR ID

Name: Mike Phillips

Likes: Cricket, books and my comfy chair.

Dislikes: Exercise, vegetables and sand in my shorts.

3 words that best describe me:
Short, round, fun.

A secret that not many people know:
Don't tell anyone, but under my hat I've got no hair!!

Visit Hilary's website at:
www.hilarymckay.co.uk

Contents

Chapter 1
Four Boys

In Peter's class there were twenty girls and four boys.

When there are only four boys and twenty girls the four boys have no choice. They have to be friends. Two friends and two left over is not good. Three friends and one left over is even worse.

It has to be all four friends together.

That's the only way that things can be happy.

The names of the boys in Peter's class were Greg, Sam, Jacob and, of course, Peter.

Greg had red hair and a basketball that he bounced as he walked.

Sam had a drum kit that he made out of boxes.

Jacob sang like an angel and went everywhere by skateboard.

They were all very noisy. As well as bouncing and drumming and singing Greg and Sam and Jacob talked all the time. They were always having adventures. When Greg and Sam and Jacob were around, even boring everyday things like shopping turned wild and amazing. They told each other the stories afterwards.

Like this –

"I saw this man and I knew he was a spy! He had dark glasses and one of those big umbrellas with daggers in their tips ..."

And this –

"There was a dog I met. He was tied up outside. He was reading the posters, I promise he was ..."

And this –

"You know the way they stack jars in the supermarket? They pile them up like towers? Well, there was a tomato sauce tower ... I don't think it was very strong and ..."

And this –

"We drove past a black shed place that had a sign that said:

BODY PARTS AND REPAIRS

... and my little sister who has just learned to read started screaming ..."

And often this –

"... So then I was totally lost!"

Greg and Sam and Jacob told stories like that all the time. They were always saying, "You'll never guess what happened to me!" They were always bursting with jokes and ideas.

That was what Greg and Sam and Jacob were like.

But it wasn't what Peter was like.

Peter was the one who never said anything. He was the quiet one.

Peter was so quiet that Greg and Sam and Jacob didn't know what to do with him.

He never had adventures.

He never rushed in to school and said, "Guess what happened to me!"

He never did drumming on boxes, or zoomed on skateboards or played basketball.

He never said, "Listen! I've had an idea!"

"I don't have ideas," said Peter.

When the others told jokes, Peter listened and smiled, but he never told one himself.

"I can't tell jokes because I never remember how they go," said Peter.

He never said anything much.

"I can never think of anything much to say," said Peter.

"What goes on in Peter's head?" the girls sometimes asked.

And Greg and Sam and Jacob had to admit, "You never know. You just can't guess.

It could be ...

nothing."

Sam and Greg and Jacob never said, "Peter is boring."

They never said it, and they never thought it.

But Peter thought it. He said it too.

"I'm boring," said Peter.

"I'm totally boring."

"I'm *amazingly* boring."

He looked round at Greg and Sam and Jacob.

Greg was shouting, "Everyone come and look at this picture I took of my Gran. I promise you, this is the photo that broke my camera!"

Sam was looking in his lunch box and asking, "Does anyone dare eat a bit of this cookie?"

Jacob had pulled off his sock and was saying, "Sniff that! It's awful, isn't it?"

Peter looked at the photo and sniffed the sock Jacob pushed under his nose and shook his head at Sam's cookie.

He didn't say much.

He never did say much.

He kept himself quiet and private.

That way, Peter thought, Greg and Sam and Jacob would never know how totally and amazingly boring he was.

****

Sometimes it did not feel like four friends to Peter.

He knew that Greg and Sam and Jacob didn't mean it.

But it felt like three and one left over.

Chapter 2
Birthday Parties

When it was not school Peter had a very easy way to keep quiet and private from Sam and Greg and Jacob. He never invited them round to his house. Sometimes they invited him to their houses. Then he would say, "Thank you," and be very polite but not go.

It was rather a lonely way to be, but at least there was no fuss.

School was not quiet at all. In a class with twenty girls and Sam and Greg and Jacob there was always something going on. Trips and plays. Sports days and birthdays.

Birthdays were the worst.

Birthdays were Peter's big problem.

Birthdays meant birthday parties.

Peter couldn't get out of the birthday parties. You can't be polite and say "Thank you" to a birthday party invitation and then not go.

Peter hated parties. He always felt more boring at birthday parties than anywhere else.

If you have three friends, that's three birthday parties a year that you have to go to. Plus your own, which makes four.

"Do I have to have a party?" Peter asked his mother every year.

"Of course you do," she said. "Sam and Greg and Jacob have parties. Why not you as well?"

"It'll be boring," said Peter. "Can't I have a year off?"

Peter's mother groaned the way she always groaned when Peter asked this question and she said, "No Peter, you're going to have a party like everyone else!"

She said that every year.

At Peter's school the party fashions changed all the time. So far Peter and Jacob and Sam and Greg had had –

Ball pit Parties

Picnic Parties

Cinema Parties

and one lovely year, Peter's favourite of all –

No Parties at all because all the boys got tummy bugs, one after the other.

At least, thought Peter, *all those parties had been somewhere else. They hadn't been parties in your own house.* Pete didn't want Greg and Sam and Jacob to see his own very boring house.

But this year the girls had started a terrible new fashion.

Sleepover Parties!

"What could be better?" asked Peter's mum.

"What could be worse?" asked Peter.

Sleepover parties came with invitations that said:

Come to my Party!

Please bring:

A sleeping bag

A tooth-brush

Pyjamas

And your phone number written down in case you suddenly want to go home in the middle of the night.

As well as these things people took –

Joke books

Midnight feast food

Tricks from the Trick Shop

Secret teddy bears.

Sleepover parties, the girls said, were the best sort of parties there ever could be. The most exciting. The most fun. The most amazing and not-boring.

So far, said the girls, no one had wanted to go home in the middle of the night.

Chapter 3
Greg's Sleepover

Greg was the first of the boys to have a sleepover party.

"Come to my party!" he yelled as he ran into the playground.

"Who?" asked Jacob.

"All of you!" said Greg. He bounced the ball off the back of Sam's head. "Here Pete, catch!" he shouted.

Peter missed (as always) and ran after the ball as it rolled away. By the time he got back Greg was saying, "You'll see my gran! Not my normal gran, the other one! Yes! The one that broke my camera! The one with the hairy chin!"

"A bit hairy or very hairy?" asked Sam.

"Very," said Greg.

"I don't think she can be as hairy as mine," said Sam. "We call my gran Big Gran. Big Gran doesn't just have a hairy chin. She's got eyebrows that join up in the middle as well!"

"Join up in the middle?" asked Peter. "Eyebrows that join up in the middle?"

"My Big Gran's eyebrows," Sam went on, "are just one huge black fuzzy line. Like a monkey's tail. Stuck on."

"WELL," said Jacob, "We call my gran Granbags and she SHAVES her hairy chin and HIDES her joined-up eyebrows under a big red hat AND she has grey furry legs just like the BIG BAD WOLF."

Peter's mouth fell open at the thought of this amazing gran but he couldn't think of a single thing to say. His gran, he was sure, wasn't any more hairy than any other old lady.

Unless there was something he hadn't noticed.

Just in case, on his way home from school, Peter stopped at his gran's house and had a good hard look at her.

Her eyebrows were drawn on with pencil.

Her chin was as bare as a plastic bag.

Her legs were as smooth as bananas.

Peter was very glad that Sam and Jacob and Greg couldn't see her.

He was very fed up.

He was even more fed up when he went to Greg's sleepover and saw Greg's gran, the one that broke Greg's camera, the one with the hairy chin.

She was the most exciting thing at the party.

My gran, thought Peter to himself in the middle of the night, *is boring*.

Like me.

Then he snuffled a bit and wished he could go home, but he couldn't because it was the middle of the night.

No one ever went home from sleepovers in the middle of the night, no matter what it said on the invitations.

Chapter 4
Sam's Sleepover

Sam was the next of them to have a birthday.

"Come to my party!" said Sam. He thundered into the playground with his new birthday bongo drums under one arm. "Come to my party but bring your own food if you like because my dad'll be doing the cooking. Here, have a bash on my new drums, Pete! ... Harder than that! Harder than that! Harder than that! Oh, don't bother!"

"What's the matter with your dad's cooking?" asked Peter as he handed back the bongo drums as quickly as he could.

"My dad," Sam went on, "is an Awful Cook. His cooking is Black. My dad makes Black Pancakes. In fact, he can *only* make Black Pancakes. And when he's made them he says, 'Eat them up! Eat them up! Black is good for you!'"

"Well that's better than my dad," said Greg. He turned his basketball into a bongo drum to be the same as Sam. "Black Pancakes sound pretty good cooking to me. Once my dad made my mum a birthday cake. And in the cake, all mixed up and cooked, we found a wodge of kitchen roll and all the candle holders AND the cat's old collar!"

"The real cat's real collar?" asked Peter.

"The real cat's real collar with bells on!" said Greg.

"That's nothing," said Jacob. "*My* mum makes OLD BONE SOUP!"

"*What?*" shouted everyone.

"She gets old bones ..." Jacob started to say.

"*How old?*" they shouted.

"Really old! She gets really old bones from her old bone bag ..."

"Your mum has an old bone bag?" asked Peter.

"I promise you my mum has an old bone bag," said Jacob. "She gets them from inside roast chickens and she keeps them in the freezer and when she's got lots of them she boils them up for soup. Old Bone Soup!"

"*What* does it taste like?" asked Sam and Greg and Peter.

"It tastes terrible!" said Jacob. "It tastes *awful*. It tastes like OLD BONE SOUP!"

Peter walked home trying and trying to think of a story worse than the black pancake story and the birthday cake story and the Old Bone Soup story and he couldn't. His mum's cakes had nothing exciting mixed up inside them, her pancakes were only brownish and her soup came out of tins.

It's not fair, thought Peter.

****

And then it was the day of Sam's sleepover. Sam's dad cooked pancakes that were so black that even strawberry jam and chocolate spread didn't cover up the crispy bits. And he said, just as Sam had said he would, "Eat them, eat them! I cooked them specially. Sam asked me to. And anyway, Black is Good For You."

Sam's dad's cooking was the worst that Peter had ever had.

Peter knew his mum could never make anything even half as bad. He lay awake all night thinking, *Mum is boring. Gran is boring. And I am the most boring of all.*

He was so unhappy he wished he could go home. But no one ever went home from sleepovers in the middle of the night, no matter what it said on the invitations.

Chapter 5
Jacob's Sleepover

Jacob's birthday was in November. He swooped into the playground on his skateboard and spun round Sam and Greg and Peter.

"It's my birthday at last!" he sang in a voice like an angel.

"And my sleepover tonight!

It will be fantastic – you can see my new hamster that I only got last week.

He smells so terrible that we've had to buy him his own air freshener.

He smells a bit like shoes and a bit like rubbish bins.

And a bit like fish.

But worse."

"Maybe you need to clean him out more," said Peter.

"*We clean him out every day*," sang Jacob sweetly.

"*It is the hamster that smells.*

Not the cage."

"Cleaning out doesn't always work," said Greg. "We clean out our fish all the time but the water is *always* green and *always* smells of cabbage and the faster the fish swim the worse it is. In fact you can see the fish making the brand new clean water go green."

"Well," said Sam, "Well, wait till you hear this! Our dog GLOWS in the dark!"

"*WHAT?*" shouted everyone.

"Our dog gives off a gas so strong and so stinky that he *GLOWS IN THE DARK!* And we took him to the vet because we were worried that he'd catch fire and the vet said, 'It's perfectly normal. Your dog will not catch fire but try to keep him in the shade on hot days because he may get a bit smoky'."

Then all the boys looked at Peter because it was his turn to tell a smelly pet story.

Peter looked back at them and he opened his mouth.

"What?" asked Greg. "Go on! What does your pet do?"

Peter closed his mouth again, put his hands in his pockets and walked away.

"What did we say?" asked Sam.

"Nothing," said Greg.

"What did he think we said?"

"Nothing," said Jacob.

"What is he thinking then?"

"Nothing," said Greg.

****

Jacob's sleepover was fantastic and the hamster was the star. They took him to bed with them but had to put his cage out of the room in the middle of the night because he smelled so terrible.

"Told you so!" said Jacob and opened the window.

****

Peter went home and sniffed things. He sniffed his cat and his mum and his gran who was there for tea.

"Do you think there's anything wrong with my nose?" he asked his mum.

"Why should there be?" his mum said.

"You don't smell right," explained Peter. "I mean you do smell, I'm not saying you don't smell, in fact you smell quite strong

... stronger than the cat ...

... You just don't smell ...

... Amazing.

... If you know what I mean."

"Peter, I think you've said enough," said Peter's mum, so Peter went quiet again.

Quiet.

And quieter.

And quieter still.

It was nearly his birthday.

Chapter 6
Before Peter's Sleepover

Greg and Sam and Jacob had talked about their birthdays for weeks before. Peter didn't say a word about his. He hoped they would all forget.

They didn't.

"Two weeks till your birthday Peter," said Jacob.

(Peter tried to look like he hadn't heard.)

Then, seven days later:

"One week till your birthday, Peter," said Sam.

(*As if I didn't know*, thought Peter.)

After that it was,

Six days ...

"I thought I'd cook pizza. Everyone always likes pizza," said Peter's mum.

(*Pizza*, thought Peter. *The most boring food on the planet*.)

Five days ...

"Pizza, chips, ice cream and cake. Birthday cake, of course."

(*My worst sort of cake*, thought Peter.)

"With that sort of food," said Peter's mum, "I don't think anything can go wrong."

Nothing will go wrong, thought Peter. He felt very gloomy.

"What's the matter?" asked his mum.

"I'm just trying," said Peter, "I'm just trying to remember ...

... only it's hard because you've cooked so much

... for so long

... and lots of times I just eat and don't notice ...

I'm just trying to remember the worst thing ...

... the most awful thing

.... the most disgusting thing

... you ever

... cooked."

"I don't know why I bother!" said Peter's mother.

"Don't bother," Peter put in so as to be helpful.

"I am going to bother," said Peter's mother. "And you are going to put up with it and THAT IS THAT! Now, bed!"

So Peter went to bed and when he woke up it was only four days till his birthday.

Four days ...

"Better get your bedroom tidy!" said Peter's mum.

Three days ...

"I've got a good idea," said Peter's gran. "You can bring your friends round to my house for bedtime hot chocolate. I'd like to see them."

Yes, but then they would see you, thought Peter. The thought made him so worried that he asked his gran a very difficult question.

He didn't want to ask the question, but he had to, just in case.

"Gran," said Peter. "Do you have a hairy ...

... no, forget it ...

... I'm going ...

... I only thought ... maybe ...

... so I could tell the other boys ...

... do you have a hairy...

... CHEST?"

Peter's gran said she did not have a hairy chest. She said it in a very cross way. She said other things too which Peter didn't hear because he ran away and shouted, "NO! Please don't show me!" while she was still saying them.

It got to two days ...

"I've written out the invitations," said Peter's mum.

(*I'll drop them on the way to school*, planned Peter.)

"... And I've telephoned their mothers!"

Peter groaned.

"... They all said, 'Yes, thank you, lovely!'"

And then there was only one day left and Peter had to face the fact that Greg and Sam and Jacob were coming to his house.

For a sleepover party.

Where they would meet his gran and his mum and his non-stinky cat.

And then they would know for ever and ever how totally boring he was.

And there was nothing he could do to stop it.

Chapter 7
Peter's Sleepover

That afternoon Greg and Sam and Jacob all came home from school with Peter. They drummed and bounced and skate-boarded and talked all the way. They were bursting with excitement. They raced upstairs to Peter's room, unrolled their sleeping bags, pumped up their air beds and hid away their teddy bears.

They were almost fizzing as they stroked the cat and ate their pizza and chips and ice cream and birthday cake.

Then they explored the house, went a bit wild when they watched a dinosaur DVD and clattered off to Peter's gran's. They told jokes all the way there. The hot chocolate made them even more cheerful. They came roaring back like drunks.

They were very polite. No one said "Your gran's not very hairy," or "Your cat doesn't smell much," or "Your mum's cooking isn't that exciting," or anything rude. Peter's mum and Peter's gran said, "What lovely boys!"

But all the time Peter had the feeling that his friends were waiting for something more to happen. Like the feeling when the sky is dark with snow clouds and one snowflake has fallen and you know for sure there are a million more to come.

And he was right.

They were.

At bedtime, as they lay in a tidy line on Peter's floor they said:

"We've all got torches in case we're going looking for secret passages."

"We could climb out of the window if you're planning to dig for treasure."

"Is this one of those houses where you can get onto the roof?"

"What's going to happen now?"

"When will it begin?"

And Peter had to say,

"Nothing's going to happen now. Nothing's going to begin. I'm very sorry but there aren't any secret passages. I've already hunted all round the garden and there isn't any treasure. It isn't one of those houses where you can get out onto the roof. The ghost's just a little bit see-through and not at all scary."

"The ghost?" asked Sam and Jacob and Greg. "WHAT GHOST?"

"Oh, just a normal sort of ghost," said Peter. "If you know what I mean."

"Do you mean," asked Sam, "the sort of ghost, that slides ever so softly from under your bed when you are half asleep and waits with its face close to yours until you feel the cold air ... the freezing breath ... the dead breath on your skin ... and when you open your eyes, his eyes are staring right into yours and you can see inside his head and it is *darkness darkness darkness!* Then you faint. Is that the sort of ghost you mean?"

"No," said Peter. "I'm sorry. I'm really sorry, Sam, but that isn't the sort I mean."

"Well, do you mean the sort of ghost," said Greg, "who PUSHES open the door BANG and all the lights come on and flash GREEN and explode and you're suddenly in TOTAL BLACKNESS and you scream and the sound of your scream is silence and you jump up and run and when you run he's always in front and you can't escape and it's HORRIBLE HORRIBLE HORRIBLE and when you come round you're flat on the floor and the room's smashed to bits and the window's wide open and the curtains are flapping and it's like a windstorm just stopped. Do you mean that sort of ghost?"

"No," said Peter, feeling awful. "I can see that would be good, Greg. I can see that would be really good, but I didn't mean anything a bit like that."

Jacob stood up and held a torch under his chin. "I suppose," said Jacob, "what you mean is the sort of ghost that you hear first, footsteps coming nearer and nearer to your bedroom door and you think GO PAST GO PAST OH DON'T STOP HERE but they do, and very slowly the door creaks wider and wider open until you can see a SHAPE, and the SHAPE has a head all flopped sideways because its neck is broken and it's wrapped in white-ish yellow-ish bandages round and round to hold its bones together, and it takes off the bandages and its jaw drops down and its ribs fall out like sticks, and it rattles words at you out of the black hole that's its mouth in a voice like stones grinding together, and the words it says are I WILL BIND YOU I WILL BIND YOU I WILL BIND YOU."

When Peter could talk again, (he'd nearly died of fright), he said, "No, Jacob. It's a pity,

I know it's boring, but I didn't mean anything at all like that."

A polite silence filled the room. Polite but a bit fed up too.

Chapter 8
Peter's Surprise

The polite silence was broken by the sound of humming.

Soft, slow, moaning humming.

Getting closer, so you could hear the tune.

'Happy Birthday' from another world.

And through the door drifted Peter's ghost.

He was not at all like the ghosts that Sam and Greg and Jacob had talked about. He drifted like smoke through the door and murmured, "Excuse me. I'll just pull myself together!" Then he turned round so as to put his head on his neck more neatly. After that he put his not very blood-stained sword carefully away and flicked his cloak around him to cover the worst of the blood. The ghost was so busy humming and fussing that at first he did not see Sam and Greg and Jacob.

When he did, he jumped.

"Dear me!" he said, as he floated up above Peter and his friends. "A party! I'm so sorry! What must you think? Shall I vanish?"

"Oh no, please don't go!" said Peter. "Stay and meet my friends first. They all love ghosts, they've just been telling me! This is Sam."

"Sam," the ghost said, and stooped politely over Sam. He held out a cold pale hand and waited for Sam to shake it.

"Oh!" cried Sam. "Oh it's a dream, it's a dream, oh promise it's a dream! OH! IT TOUCHED ME!"

"And that's Greg, next to Sam," Peter went on with a grin at Sam because Sam had been so good at acting as if he was really scared.

"I don't believe in ghosts," said Greg. He sat right up and talked very fast. "I really don't. I won't. They're shadows. They're your imagination. They're nothing at all! DON'T COME NEAR! DON'T COME NEAR! DON'T COME NEAR!"

(*Greg's good at acting too*, thought Peter. *Just like that with no practice! If you didn't know you'd think he was scared to death.*)

"And this is Jacob," Peter said.

Jacob had already begun to act as if he was scared, and he was doing just as well as Sam and Greg. He was breathing in a very odd way, in and out very hard, making a small creaking noise, like a little panting donkey. When the ghost turned round to say hello to him he flung himself flat under his pillow and yelled "GET THE OTHERS! GET THE OTHERS! GET THE OTHERS! LEAVE ME ALONE!"

"Your friends," said the ghost, turning to Peter, "are perhaps very very rude …"

"My mum and my gran," said Peter, "think they're very polite."

"… or else very very shy!" the ghost finished off.

"Oh no," said Peter, and he tried not to smile. "They're very brave in real life!"

"If you say so," said the ghost, but he looked as if he didn't believe a word of it. "I have to admit Real Life is not for me these days, nor has been for the last three hundred years. However, it was you I came to see. I wanted to wish you many Happy Returns of the Day ..."

"Oh, thank you," Peter said.

"I say 'Returns' but I don't know if you *will* get more birthdays or not. Stay out of sword fights, that's my advice."

"I will do," said Peter.

"Do not lose your temper with robbers ... easier said than done, I admit ..."

"I'll try," said Peter.

"And don't go slashing around with daggers on dark nights. It's only fun for the first few minutes."

"I suppose ..." Peter started to say.

"Now, don't argue, Peter!" snapped the ghost. "I speak because I know these things! Now promise!"

"I promise I won't go slashing about with daggers on dark nights," said Peter meekly.

"It's for his own good," explained the ghost to Sam, Greg and Jacob. "He's always taking terrible risks. You must know that yourselves."

Sam, Greg and Jacob nodded. They sat, with huge round eyes, in the grey ghost light.

"Now I must be off," the ghost said. "Places to visit. Things to do. But first a card for Peter! I know I put it somewhere!"

The ghost hunted around under his cloak and Greg, Sam and Jacob saw such a horrible black hole that it made them moan and cover their eyes.

"They're scared of blood, I expect," said the ghost.

"It does look sore," said Peter.

"Doesn't hurt a bit," said the ghost. "The sword went right into me. Just as I was cutting his ... well, never mind! Ah! Here it is! Your card!"

"Thank you very much," said Peter.

"... F-F-F-F-F-Fancy a ghost giving a birthday card!" stammered Greg in surprise.

"Not birthday, Death day!" corrected the ghost who was now slowly floating backwards through the door. "Death day! Silly boy! Still, can't expect old heads on young shoulders. Or any heads on any shoulders sometimes," he added and took off his own head. "Don't

forget my warning, Peter! No sword fights after bedtime! Good night!"

"Good night!" said Peter. "And thank you! Oh, he's gone! I'll put the light on then, if that's OK. Just for a minute, so that I can read my card."

"Put it on for as long as you like," said Sam as he pulled his sleeping bag up around him. So Peter hopped out of bed and flicked the switch by the door, and the room suddenly filled with light. Sam, Greg and Jacob began to look much better.

"Gosh!" said Jacob in a shaky voice. "So that was really your real ghost, Peter?"

"Mmm," nodded Peter and ripped open his envelope (which was black). "He's nice, isn't he? I mean, I know he'd be better if he did more banging and flashing and grabbing and yelling like you were saying before. But he can't seem to do the really good stuff. Still,

I think he tries. You all did very good pretending."

"Pretending?" said Sam as he slowly came back to normal. "What do you mean, pretending?"

"Like you were scared," explained Peter.

"Like we were scared?" asked Greg, still rather trembly but getting better. "That wasn't scared!"

"That was terrified," said Jacob in a grim voice.

"Very, very terrified!" said Greg.

Sam nodded.

"Oh!" said Peter. "Oh, I'm sorry! I thought you were just doing it to be nice! Shall I get my mum? Do you want to telephone your families? Are you all suddenly going home? It's the middle of the night!"

"Home?" asked Greg.

"We love it here!" said Sam.

"It's fantastic!" agreed Jacob.

"What's more," added Jacob. "It doesn't matter what happens at sleepovers, no one ever really goes home in the middle of the night! Let's see your card, Pete!"

Peter passed round his card. It was a picture of a grey gravestone with a green glowing patch which said:

Scratch with a coin here to find out the day you will die.

His friends passed it round and were careful not to touch the green patch. Peter hunted under his bed for his money box and began to shake it.

"Peter!" said Greg.

"I need a coin," explained Peter. He found a ten-pence coin and began to scratch the green patch on his card. "Oh, boring!"

"Boring?" said Sam and Greg and Jacob.

"Same day as last year," said Peter. "I think he gets those cards cheap."

Sam and Greg and Jacob looked at each other, and then at Peter, who was sitting up in his bed in his blue stripy pyjamas. The boy who was friends with a ghost. The boy who had to be warned not to slash around with daggers in the dark. Who wasn't at all scared about opening Death Day cards. Who didn't seem to care about blood or heads that came off or anything else ...

"Why didn't you tell us?" they asked.

"Tell you what?" asked Peter. He was turning over his card to look at the back in case the ghost had left the price on by mistake.

"Well, about your ghost, for one thing!" they all said.

"Why would I?" asked Peter. "He's just a normal sort of ghost, like my gran is a normal sort of gran, and my cat is a normal sort of cat and my mum's cooking is normal sort of boring cooking ..."

"Yes, well, about your gran," said Jacob. "That's another thing you didn't tell us! She's not normal. In fact, I don't want to be rude, Pete, but your gran is almost *bald*."

"And about your cat," said Sam. "He's not what I'd call normal. Hadn't you noticed that your cat has *nearly no smell at all?*"

"And didn't you know," asked Greg, "that your mum is PROBABLY THE BEST COOK IN THE WORLD?"

"Oh yes," admitted Peter. "I knew all that."

"Well, you didn't tell us!"

"I just didn't think it was important."

The boys looked at each other and shook their heads and said, "Amazing!"

"What's amazing?" asked Peter, and they all said,

"YOU!"

****

After that Sam and Greg and Jacob always had an answer if people asked them about their quiet friend who never said much.

If anyone asked, "What goes in Peter's head?"

They always said proudly, "You never know ...

... You just can't say ...

... It could be ...

... ANYTHING!"

Barrington Stoke would like to thank all its readers for commenting on the manuscript before publication and in particular:

Laura Anderson
Sarah Andrews
Joe Baxter
Matthew Bryant
Sophie Bugg
Bethany Bunn
Judy Carter-Brown
Catherine Clancy
Charles Clay
Sarah Coupland
Lauren Cox
Anna Davies
Adam Driver
Laura Edwards
Helen Fagg
Rosalind Faulkner
Tom Fewlass
Jack Flynn
Kate Gollogly
Isobel Goudie
Gemma Harrison
Faye Holland
Anna Holt
Abbie Howard
Jade Hunt
Laura Jackson
Darrell Houghton Judge
Susan Kaye
Danielle Lisbon
Reece M.
Angeline Maher
Thomas May
Amie Metcalfe
Emma Milner
Emma Moorish
Sarah Moxon
Neil Musk
Becky Privett
Emily Pywell
Josh R.
Jessamyn Read
Elizabeth Reece
Gemma Richardson
Faye Watson
Francesca Watson
Bria Williamson

Become a Consultant!

Would you like to give us feedback on our titles before they are published? Contact us at the email address below – we'd love to hear from you!

info@barringtonstoke.co.uk
www.barringtonstoke.co.uk

Great reads – no problem!

Barrington Stoke books are:

Great stories – from thrillers to comedy to horror, and all by the best writers around!

No hassle – fast reads with no boring bits, and a story that doesn't let go of you till the last page.

Short – the perfect size for a fast, fun read.

We use our own font and paper to make it easier to read our books. And we ask teenagers like you, who want a no-hassle read, to check every book before it's published.

That way, we know for sure that every Barrington Stoke book is a great read for everyone.

Check out www.barringtonstoke.co.uk for more info about Barrington Stoke and our books!

Also by the same author ...

Dragon!

When Max won't tidy his room, his Witchy Aunt flies off in a temper – on her broomstick! Max is left on his own, with a dragon's egg to look after! But now the dragon's coming out ... and it's hungry!

You can order *Dragon!* directly from our website at **www.barringtonstoke.co.uk**